CHOOSING ELEONORE

ESSENTIAL TRANSLATIONS SERIES 52

Canada

ONTARIO ARTS COUNCIL
CONSEIL DES ARTS DE L'ONTARIO

an Ontario government agency
un organisme du gouvernement de l'Ontario

Canada Council   Conseil des Arts
for the Arts   du Canada

Guernica Editions Inc. acknowledges the support of the Canada
Council for the Arts and the Ontario Arts Council.
The Ontario Arts Council is an agency of the Government of Ontario.
We acknowledge the financial support of the Government of Canada.
Nous reconnaissons l'appui financier du gouvernement du Canada.

CHOOSING ELEONORE

ANDRÉE A. GRATTON

Translated by Ian Thomas Shaw

GUERNICA
TORONTO—CHICAGO—BUFFALO—LANCASTER
2021

Original title: *Choisir Éléonore* (2015)
Copyright © 2015, Les éditions de la Pleine Lune
Translation copyright © 2021 Ian Thomas Shaw and Guernica Editions
Inc.

Michael Mirolla, editor
Cover art Element AI mural by Ola Volo
Cover and interior design Ian Thomas Shaw
Guernica Editions Inc.
287 Templemead Drive, Hamilton (ON), Canada L8W 2W4
2250 Military Road, Tonawanda, N.Y. 14150-6000 U.S.A.
www.guernicaeditions.com
Distributors
Independent Publishers Group (IPG)
600 North Pulaski Road, Chicago IL 60624
University of Toronto Press Distribution,
5201 Dufferin Street, Toronto (ON), Canada M3H 5T8
Gazelle Book Services, White Cross Mills
High Town, Lancaster LA1 4XS U.K.
First edition
Printed in Canada.
Legal Deposit—Third Quarter
Library of Congress Catalog Card Number: 2020942168
Library and Archives Canada Cataloguing in Publication
Title: Choosing Eleonore / Andrée A. Gratton ; translated by Ian
Thomas Shaw.
Other titles: Choisir Éléonore.
English Names: Gratton, Andrée-Anne, 1980– author. | Shaw, Ian
Thomas, 1955– translator.
Series: Essential translations series ; 52.
Description: Series statement: Essential translations series ; 52 |
Translation of: Choisir Éléonore.
Identifiers: Canadiana 20200290789 | ISBN 9781771836500
(softcover)
Classification: LCC PS8563.R3797 C5613 2021 | DDC C843/.6—
dc23

To Catherine

If I'm urged to say why I loved him,
I feel that this can only be expressed by answering:
"Because it was him, because it was me."
—**Montaigne**, *Essais*

CHAPTER ONE

LONG BEFORE WE MET, Eleonore was dreaming of me. Not me with this hair, these two hands or the sound of my voice. No. Of me as a friend, an ideal friend.

I saw her a year ago, at the exit of the hospital where I work. She was facing me, her back resting against a telephone booth on the other side of Avenue des Pins. Four women formed a semi-circle around her. They kept bursting out in laughter, waving their hands excitedly. I stood there, motionless in the middle of the parking lot, spying on her. No one noticed my presence, neither she nor the four other women. I could easily go unnoticed, unlike her. Me, with my green nurse's uniform; her, with her short yellow skirt and high heels.

Very quickly they appeared bored. They shut up, looked around and let out sighs, whose sullen and noisy release could only be imagined. Slowly they walked down University Street and, with small steps brushing against the pavement, headed south. I followed a few metres behind them. Eleonore was in the middle; like props, the others deferred to her passively.

At the bottom of the hill, she kissed them one by one, then alone headed southeast to the next bus stop. I slipped in on her right into the line-up. A gold bracelet encircled her left ankle. She was taller than me, even though she had taken off her heels.

Once on board, I thought I would talk to her, tell her that we would be friends, or, simply, talk to her about the nice May weather taking hold of the city. But I didn't dare speak. She kept looking straight ahead the whole way.

We reached a neighbourhood in the city's east end. She pulled the cord two or three times and then jumped up out of her seat. There were four or five of us getting off behind her. She walked a few minutes before entering one of the tall dirty buildings on Rue Joliette. She didn't use a key. A few seconds later, I snuck inside.

I heard a door slamming on one of the upper floors, but wasn't able to identify which one. I sat on a step and waited.

I then imagined Eleonore at home: changing out of her clothes, putting on more comfortable ones; cooking something, maybe pasta; the heat and steam enveloping the kitchen and leaving a fine mist on the beige painted walls, windows and floor tiles; she opens a window; she sits on a bottle-green moleskin sofa; she turns on the television; she lights a cigarette. That's when she starts thinking about me.

This scenario emboldened me. I got up. My uniform was dirty and stuck to my buttocks and the back of my knees. I went up to the first floor. There were two apartments. I knocked on the first one, but no one answered. The door of the second one opened immediately. An old man with his shirt off asked me in a hoarse voice what I wanted. The TV was screaming behind him. I showed him the scarf I kept at the bottom of my bag.

– Does this belong to you?

– No!

And he closed the door.

From behind the only door on the second floor, she appeared. I stammered a Hello, Madam! and adopted the same tactic. But the scarf didn't belong to her. That I knew. She looked at me for a few seconds while squinting. She no longer had on her short yellow skirt but a grey terrycloth dressing gown. She wanted to close the door. I insisted, a little, on shaking her hand and wishing her a nice evening. I also showed her proof of my identity: health and social insurance cards, driving licence.

– I have been working for seven years at the reception desk of the Royal Victoria Hospital. I saw you there at the exit earlier. I'm not used to approaching strangers like this. But it's not the same with you. Do you understand? Of course! Friendship is such a rare thing …

I continued for a few seconds to talk about the virtue of friendship. Then I sort of lost track of what I was saying. She closed the door.

I waited a few minutes. I crouched down to look through the keyhole but couldn't see anything. Finally, my back against her door, I slid to the floor to listen to the sounds inside. The TV was off. Maybe she was reading. A novel, let's call it *Amours*, one that she had barely started. I heard her cough several times. I recognized the sound of the bathtub filling up. She was there for a long time. She played music—I don't know what. The silence returned.

I looked at my watch. It was after midnight. I was supposed to be in the hospital the next day at seven o'clock. I stayed there for a few more minutes, singing a sweet song, a lullaby, certain that she would like this tune.

Then a man, a stranger, came up the stairs. He stopped in front of the door, fists on his hips, looking down at me. I refused to let him pass, explaining that Eleonore was "asleep, no doubt about it." He laughed nervously. He claimed he was invited. He gradually became angry as I stubbornly refused to move. He shouted through the door to Eleonore. Growing impatient, he grabbed me under my arms, brusquely lifted me up and pushed me aside.

I fell down the stairs and lost consciousness.

I was told at the hospital that a neighbour had called the police. I received five stitches and fractured my right wrist. I filed a complaint against the stranger, on the advice of the two female police officers who had questioned me at the hospital.

When I saw Eleonore accompany the violent man to the police station two weeks later, she didn't dare look at me, probably out of shame, out of decency. So I decided to help her. I withdrew my complaint.

CHAPTER TWO

I RETURNED TO WORK after a short recovery.

At the time, I was in charge of the preliminary exam-ination of patients arriving at the ER—triage. I received them one by one in an airtight room, encased by large glass doors, nicknamed "the aquarium." I spent nine hours a day there. The patients, already worried about a long wait in the adjacent room, entered, dishevelled, wide-eyed, often distraught, sometimes with a bloody limb. They came in and explained their pain. I would nod, matched their words with uh-huh, uh-huh and then ask a series of questions.

– When was the last time you had a medical examina-tion? Are you taking any medication? Have you ever had an operation?

Sometimes, a few exchanges took place. Then the patients would inevitably return to wait for several hours in the room from where they had arrived.

The day I went back to work, it was very difficult for me not to confide everything I knew about Eleonore to the patients who seemed the most worthy to hear it. I could not keep quiet about her great generosity, strong sense of leadership and unwavering aesthetic taste.

– It is rare nowadays to meet a person of such quality, confirmed an eighty-three-year-old woman whose right arm had stopped moving more than twenty-four hours earlier.

I didn't reveal anything to my colleagues, but many of them noticed my good mood.

At the end of the day, I quickly left the aquarium. I expected to see Eleonore again in the same place as the first time. She knew where I was working, so it was easy for her to meet me there. I waited an hour and twenty minutes. The usual rush hour on Avenue des Pins: pedestrians, cars, all very anonymous and in a hurry. But there was no trace of Eleonore.

I went to her house. Before getting on the bus, I bought vegetables and cheese for the omelette she was probably going to cook that night.

Keeping my head down, I climbed up to the door of her apartment. Something massive tightened in my chest. I rang the bell once, short of breath. No noise. I rang the bell a second time. The third ring, still nothing.

I checked the groceries in the plastic bag and left them by the door. On the back of the cash register receipt, I wrote:

Hello, I came to see you, but something must have delayed you. I hope that these few ingredients will make your meal more enjoyable. It's an omelette you're making tonight, isn't it? Have a pleasant evening. See you very soon. Marianne N.

P.S. Soon, we will move onto a first-name basis ...

I slipped the message under her door, hoping that she would find it as soon as she stepped inside.

CHAPTER THREE

I CYCLED TO her place every day the following week. Using a map of the city I found in the back of a closet, I figured out the best route to get from the hospital to her apartment and back home. I needed forty minutes in the first case, one hour and twenty minutes in the second.

At 4:05 p.m., I was riding my bike, travelling at full speed to the east side of the city. I bought my evening meal every day at the local grocery store—a sandwich and some chocolate—before returning to my observation post. I didn't go up to her house to say hello, invite her out or confide in her this or that difficulty I had encountered during the day. I always sat in the same place, across the street, at a forty-five-degree angle to her windows. The warm June weather allowed me to stay this way for hours on end.

Our relationship didn't evolve much. Or rather, Eleonore learned very little about me. On the other hand, some of her habits became much clearer to me.

When I arrived, her windows would be closed despite the heat. But the curtains were open, and I could see some furtive movements inside. When daylight faded, Eleonore lit up the apartment. I could then clearly distinguish the shapes and life inside. Sometimes, she would leave the apartment unlit for several minutes. I wondered what she could be thinking about, plunged like that in darkness. Maybe the darkness was making her think of me? She must have been questioning the meaning of life, I said to myself, why she failed to keep close to her the people who cared about her, why she was still living alone.

Then she would open the windows wide, slowly poke her head outside and scan the street with a glance. Several times, I thought she saw me. But her gaze passed right through me.

She would go inside after a while, pulling a sheer curtain across the windows. Then she would play very loud, trendy, American Pop music. I knew a number of the songs by heart. Alone in the street, I would accompany her softly when she started singing at the top of her voice, drowning out the crackling of the speakers.

Shortly afterwards, I would watch the light soften, going from white to blue, pink or orange. She would half-close the windows, replacing the pop music with lustful tunes I didn't know, played at a slower and more exotic rhythm. A moment would pass before a second silhouette appeared. A man, each time different, often fat, small or tall, dressed in a suit with a tie. He would approach Eleonore with gentleness or roughness, confidence or clumsiness. Then they both would disappear. Forty minutes later, Eleonore would lean against the window, alone, smoking a cigarette, in a dressing gown. I recognized the man coming out of the building, looking severe and sneaking around the corner in a hurry.

Every night that week, the same scenario repeated itself.

CHAPTER FOUR

THE FOLLOWING SATURDAY, after getting up at half past five in the morning, showering and eating two bowls of cereal, I arrived in front of the building. It was six forty, too early to go up to her apartment. The weather was mild and bright. I decided to stay outside, waiting for her to appear.

Over the course of the morning, old people and young families began to stroll along the sidewalk. An old man came to me to talk about the nice weather. The discussion quickly turned to my relationship with Eleonore.

– It's a wonderful coincidence for both of us, I said. I can imagine what she herself would say about it.

I began to imitate Eleonore's voice to reproduce her words.

– At last! I've needed someone like Marianne so much in my life: a friend to laugh with, cry with, be bored with! It's a blessing. The best thing that could have happened to me right now.

The old man smiled. He left, his head nodding in approval.

After one o'clock, a muscular man in a white t-shirt opened the windows while talking to someone behind him. Eleonore joined him. She stroked his neck and face. They kissed. Then she was alone. She leaned her elbows against the windowsill. She closed her eyes and began to breathe in and out for a long time.

– Hello!

She opened her eyes. She shaded her eyes with her right hand from the sunlight. She looked about, trying to locate my voice.

– Hello, it's me! I repeated when she saw me.

She didn't say anything. She closed her eyes and plunged back into her breathing exercises. She didn't recognize me. She must have thought I was talking to someone else.

– Do you remember me?

She opened her eyes again but didn't look at me and then slipped back inside.

The presence of the man had to explain her attitude. She couldn't leave him alone at home while she was having a conversation with me. She couldn't be sure what he would do? Out of boredom, would he start drinking? Breaking dishes? Stealing precious objects? She was right to ignore me until he left. She could soon give me all the space I need.

He left ten hours after I arrived that morning. I tidied my hair, adjusted my shirt and jeans. I made sure there were no food stains on them. I went up to Eleonore's apartment.

With a confident fist, I knocked quickly three times on her door. I heard the wooden floor creak inside. She opened the door.

– Hello! I'm sorry I took all this time to come. But so much has happened, hasn't it?

– I don't think we know each other.

– I understand. It's been so short a time since we met. What? Barely a month? She didn't invite me to her house. She stepped back and tried to close the door.

– Wait a minute! Wait a minute! I thought we'd spend the day together. I didn't know anyone would be here with you. If you like, I can help you tidy up, do the housework, while you tell me about your day.

Her hazelnut brown eyes stared at me without blinking.

She tilted her head to the right.

To put her at ease, I told her an anecdote about a certain patient. In the middle of a sentence, she pushed me back and closed the door.

She was dignified and private. She needed to get to know people better before talking to them. I screamed through the door that I didn't blame her. On the contrary, I understood her reaction very well.

I leaned against her door. It was past five o'clock.

I sang many of the songs I had heard regularly from her apartment.

– I know you like these melodies!

Out of breath, I took out of my bag the day's paper. I started with the news, reading aloud the political, sports and cultural headlines. Quickly, I jumped to the horoscope. I asked Eleonore what her sign was.

– From what I know of you, you must be a Leo. I am Sagittarius and, good news, this month, our two signs are in sync. Listen! After reading the horoscope, I attacked the crossword puzzles. She didn't participate. They were full of little traps. I finished with the classified ads that I read in their entirety. I sometimes interrupted my reading to ask Eleonore questions, not always understanding the services being offered. Still unanswered, increasingly tired, I slipped onto the floor and fell asleep, lying like a watchdog at the foot of her closed door.

The sudden slamming of the door woke me up. It was after ten o'clock. Eleonore stepped over me without tripping. I didn't recognize her right away. Perched on red patent leather high heels, her legs in green stockings, she wore a glittering purple skirt, a narrow leather jacket and a black-crested hat.

– Where are you going?

She didn't turn around. She rushed down the stairs. I felt about for my shoes and jacket that I had pushed aside while I slept. Then I ran down the stairs. I tripped on the last step. I left the building in a state of disarray. Too late. Eleonore was no longer there.

CHAPTER FIVE

SHE COULDN'T SEE me for the next two weeks. I stayed focused on my work, rest and usual distractions. I told myself that she couldn't have it all.

I returned to her home on the last Saturday in June. That day, she opened her curtains at 11 a.m. sharp. Four hours after I arrived on the sidewalk across the street. Just this once, she was alone. She opened the windows and stuck her head out. Then she saw me.

– Hello! I said. At last, how happy I am that we meet again!

– I'm busy right now.

She disappeared.

I waited outside. She walked out of the front door of her building early that evening. I hurried to join her, dragging behind me a right leg that had fallen asleep.

– I thought you had forgotten about me! Can we call each other by our first names? Can I come with you?

She continued to walk briskly. The sound of her heels echoed down the narrow street. The sides of her canary yellow raincoat were flying behind her. My left elbow

– As long as you stay calm … Here, take my stool. It wouldn't hurt me to walk around a bit.

His kindness encouraged me.

I waited until closing time. I fell asleep several times for short moments. I woke up with a start, banging my head against the brick wall behind me.

Then Eleonore came out, at the end of a line of noisy and staggering customers. She was riveted to the body of a man I had never seen before. He was holding her by the shoulders. She had both her arms wrapped around his waist. She noticed me after I almost screamed:

– At last! I was afraid something might have happened to you!

She didn't seem surprised. She straightened her neck to whisper something in the stranger's ear. He looked at me curiously and then burst out laughing.

The doorman spotted my sister. He shook his head from left to right:

– Pffff, your sister, eh? Tough luck!

Eleonore laughed:

– Oh, yes, my sister!

She walked off, twisted in laughter as the man shooed me away like he would an alley cat.

CHAPTER SIX

I'M NOT THE kind of person who begs. Eleonore didn't respect me—too bad! She would soon regret it! She could mope alone, without my assistance.

Anyway, I had neglected a number of things I needed to get back to. My work, for example. I postponed my vacation and took every opportunity there was to do overtime. There was plenty during this period since my colleagues wanted to enjoy the warm July weather. I was going to make a lot of money. This would allow me to improve some aspects of my daily life. I noticed in Eleonore's apartment a pretty shade of red on the walls. I certainly could have found this colour by myself, but Eleonore had made it easier for me. I bought some paint and spent a few days decorating my living and dining rooms.

By chance, while shopping, I came across the album that Eleonore had been listening to at her place. I bought it and played it during my renovation work. I memorized the melodies and lyrics. I also sang the songs with all my might. After all, these hits did not belong to Eleonore. I had the right to enjoy them too! Just like those light veil curtains she had installed for her windows, the candles she used to burn on weekday evenings. Just like that habit of sticking her head out of the window and scanning the street with her eyes, meditating, a glass in her hand. No, Eleonore didn't have a monopoly. I was entitled to it too!

At work, a colleague noticed my changing mood with patients. She noted the unusual and irritated nature of the remarks I made at lunchtime. She blamed it on the overload of work I had imposed on myself. She approached me, put one hand on my shoulder and insisted I take a day or two off.

– I'll be happy to replace you, don't worry.

I felt the need to confide everything to her: the friendship and its risks; the need for friends to respect a code of honour; the blindness of one to the suffering of the other; indifference; cruelty … I got carried away. That's what I realized when I saw the look on her face.

– You've never experienced this before? I asked.

– Certainly not with a friend, she replied.

I always knew I was more passionate than she was.

She asked me the name of this person "who claimed to be my friend." I didn't feel the strength to betray Eleonore. Despite what she had done to me, my desire to protect her was all the more important. I kept my mouth shut.

Five weeks went by like this.

CHAPTER SEVEN

THEN, ONE MORNING in late July, I came across a patient lying on a stretcher in the hospital corridor. The right side of her face was bloody. She twisted in pain, both hands pressed together on her abdomen. Her hair spread out on the pillow like wet, overcooked spaghetti. I bent over her, looked at her swollen and purple eyes.

– Eleonore, there you are at last! I'll take care of you, don't worry, I said in a low, excited voice.

I stroked her hair, whispered soothing words, tried to clean her wounds myself. She struggled and mumbled strange words, interspersed with weak cries of pain. I drew nearer to better understand what she was trying to say. She shook her head and whispered that I was mistaken, that her name was not Eleonore.

– You're confused by the pain. Let me take care of you. I'll get a doctor and tell him you're my best friend. Let's get you taken care of as soon as possible …

The doctor found her bunched up in the foetal position. He grabbed the medical file at the foot of her bed.

– Judith Gagnon, residing in Outremont. So your best friend lives next door to me; maybe I'll see you there one day!

It wasn't Eleonore. It was a sign from Eleonore that I should return to her.

CHAPTER EIGHT

I DIDN'T KNOW her family name. Eleonore who? The last name had to be written on her mailbox at the entrance of the building. Why didn't I think of that before?

Nine p.m. I was afraid of her reaction if she saw me hanging around. I put on some old black jeans, a baseball cap and a grey kangaroo sweatshirt. I went to her house. On the way, I promised myself I wouldn't stop. Not even to take a look at her apartment. I would walk straight to the building, enter it, as if nothing had happened, note her name down and then leave unnoticed.

An hour and fifteen minutes later, I learned that her name was Eleonore Brome.

I rushed to the first working phone booth. The operator gave me a number. I breathed slowly, deeply, and dialled it.

On the fourth ring, a man's voice answered. I was surprised that Eleonore would let a stranger use her phone. I waited a few seconds, silently.

– Hello? Hello? Hello?

He hung up. I dialled the number once again. It was him again. Behind his exasperated voice, I heard Eleonore's voice, almost shouting.

– Who is it? Who is it?

What a comfort to hear her! I wanted to say hello, tell her not to worry. But he hung up. Pleased with this renewed closeness, I went home with a light heart.

CHAPTER NINE

SHE PROBABLY WANTED to tell me about the latest events in her life. For example, her relationship with the stranger on the phone. Or the future vacation she was going to take, maybe with me.

All these weeks apart from each other meant long and deep recollections. I had to find a way to make her talk, to open up, to confide. I was hoping that a telephone conversation, despite its blanks and very long silences, despite my voice twisting in the transmission and arriving all distorted, unnatural to Eleonore's ears, would allow this opening.

I redialled her number when I got home. She answered immediately.

– It's me! I wanted to know if you needed to talk. You know I'm here for you.

I heard breathing, barely. She hung up.

I pressed redial. The line was busy. I counted to thirty and again redialled. The same puncture-proof beep beep continued for another hour. She must have dropped the handset. It was better to wait until she noticed it the next

day while cleaning the living room and probably anticip-
ating our next conversation.

So I waited until the next day. When I got back from
work, I had the whole late afternoon plus the evening to
call Eleonore and chat with her. I prepared some food.

To get rid of the day's anxiety, I listened to the music
we both liked. I did breathing exercises and some
stretching too, a few dance steps in the living room,
kitchen, bedroom. I was surprised by my reflection in
the mirror. I looked for a resemblance to Eleonore in it.
My round face, the blurry shapes of my buttocks and
belly, my salt and pepper hair—any physical similarity
between us was excluded. But our souls had been cast in
the same mould. It was obvious.

I pick up the phone. Three hours of repeated calls,
interspersed with five-minute breaks. She finally
answered. She knew it was me.

– What do you want? Just tell me once and for all!

I took a moment to respond, hoping to give a calm and
accurate answer.

– I'm calling you so we can spend some time together.
And to listen to you.

I wanted her to be more comfortable. I started talking
about myself. I told her about what had happened since
we last met: the patients, my meals, the vivid impression
that our dinner at the restaurant had left. I didn't mention
how stupid I thought the stranger in the bar was. I subtly
raised the upcoming holidays. I dared to ask my first
question:

– Would you come with me to the beach?

I repeated my question in a different way. Only the sound of a heavy and hard sole on the wooden floor answered me. Movements in a kitchen, hands looking through the clutter of a drawer.

– Eleonore?

She had put down the phone.

I had to keep quiet and pay attention to her gestures, to the sound of her movements. It was her way of inviting me to be with her. A new step towards a strong and constant friendship.

It lasted more than three hours. She played music. I heard and imagined the change of her shoes, the flat soles that turn into stiletto heels. The microwave oven. The pages of the newspaper that turned slowly while munching on a sandwich. The last look in the mirror. A touch-up of eye shadow. Lipstick. A good night and, finally, an extended beep.

We followed the same ritual for the next nine days. I called at exactly the same time every night. She carefully honoured our appointment. She let me sit in the living room, by her side, and participate in the preparations for her evening. She whispered good night each time before hanging up. Eleonore had a gift for creating strong moments of intimacy.

CHAPTER TEN

SHE'S NOT THE one who picked up on the tenth night. It was another woman. I was not prepared for such a reversal in the way we did things. A higher-pitched and less soft voice, less beautiful. Amazed, I had her repeat herself twice. Behind her, several voices mixed in.

– Eleonore?

– Ele-what?

She laughed before shouting at others:

– Eleonore. Is there anyone here by that name?

Laughter broke out. Eleonore's voice drowned out everyone else's. She asked the woman on the phone to cover the handset. All I could hear was a rumbling of air. I believe that Eleonore had confided in them the ups-and-downs and importance of our story. A few seconds later, the woman took the phone back. With a softer, trembling voice, she said:

– Yes, I apologize for keeping you waiting. Eleonore, as you call her, is busy right now. She can't talk to you, but she says you can come by. There's a little party here, so come join us.

All kinds of preparations made me arrive much later than I would have liked. I stuck my left ear against the door without hearing anything behind it—as if everyone was asleep. I rang the bell, a tall, very skinny woman with red-dyed hair opened the door immediately. Her eyes were half-closed and she looked at me with a strange look, the corner of her mouth at a slant.

– Eleonore invited me.

Her smile widened. She bit her lips.

– She's out for a few minutes, but she'll be back. Come in!

I wish Eleonore had welcomed me. I took two steps forward. On the right was a kind of living room. Uglier than I had imagined. A large brown fake leather sofa lost in a corner, facing two metal chairs. Strangers were lying on it. Others were sitting cross-legged on the wooden floor. No one was talking. Everyone had their eyes barely open, their heads turned towards the TV at the back of the room, a bottle of beer or a cigarette in their hands. I could not have foreseen such apathy among Eleonore's friends.

Only one looked up at me.

– Come sit with us while you wait for her to come back.

His voice was grainy. He patted the free spot next to him. I went there.

I thought it was strange that I wasn't asked more about my relationship with Eleonore.

– I suppose you all know my first name?

A negligible reaction.

– It doesn't matter! Can you tell me your names?

They mumbled their first names. I caught my neighbour's name: "Simon." The two women with dyed red hair slouched across from me remained anonymous.

– Have you two known each other for a long time? I asked them.

I didn't give them time to answer. I continued.

– I have only known Eleonore for a short time, but as they say, the important thing is quality, not quantity!

The TV host continued to explain how to cook *poulet chasseur*.

– All I have to do is hear her voice on the phone to know if something is wrong. No need to discuss things for long to be aware of what is happening to either of us … a simple glance, a simple word. That's also the case for both of you, isn't it?

One of the two red-haired women turned to me frowning. Something seemed to be preventing them from speaking to me. Next to me, Simon, fat and stinking, was trying to talk to me. He disgusted me so much that I didn't pay attention to him.

I left them to their little business. I sat a few steps behind them at the dining room table. I was the only person there who was worthy of Eleonore. The others enjoyed her hospitality without caring about her. I didn't dirty anything. I didn't move anything. I respected everything about my friend.

After a long time, it became difficult for me to keep my eyes open. The sound of the TV started to blur, so did the images on it. I fell asleep, my left cheek resting against the cold metal of the table.

I started dreaming about the two of us.

She and I are in the middle of a large flat field, lost in the tall, golden grass. The shade of maples and willows cools down a bit the intense heat. We are at her home, at the family residence.

Dozens of people appear in the distance. They walk towards us, with a bounce to their gait. A good mood begins to circulate, to become more and more radiant. At my side, Eleonore smiles. She is looking forward to introducing me to everyone coming toward us.

A group of musicians appears behind us. Two guitarists and a clarinet player. One of them, very happy, says to me: "So it's you! I'm glad to finally meet you. Eleonore has told me so much about you! I hope you will have a good time with us!"

He takes me very gently by the waist and leads me into a whirling dance, not taking his eyes off me. He whispers in my ear: "Thank you for all you have done for her. We are very grateful."

Her mother and father hug me more than once. Her mother is moved to tears. Her father laughs joyfully as he pats me on the back, repeating: "Oh yes! I knew it! Oh yes, I knew it!"

Eleonore takes refuge in his arms for a few moments, shedding tears of relief.

Eleonore's old friends are approaching me. They want to have time alone with me. "How lucky Eleonore is to be with you," they whisper in my ear. Eleonore walks up

31

to them and asks them to leave me alone, that we are not here for that, that they will tire me out if they continue like this.

Everything begins to move faster. I feel that people are looking for me, that they want me. They are cheering for me, hugging me, confiding in me, envying me, exalting me, I am the star of the evening.

Then the noise of a crash breaks the sky and the party.

Everything vanishes.

I woke up. A puddle of saliva had flowed from my smile while I slept, soaking the table and my cheek.

It was early in the morning. There was not a trace of last night's guests. The TV was still turned on. A young Leonardo Di Caprio appeared on it, breaking dishes on the floor in a small kitchen.

Sounds could be heard from the back. Grunts and laughter. I decided to explore the rest of the apartment. Eleonore would understand my curiosity. It was better if I let her know I was here. Ready to help her in the thankless task of cleaning up all the mess left by the others last night.

The kitchen extended backwards into a long corridor. Three doors were aligned there. The first one opened on a cupboard stacked with towels, brooms, vials of medicine. The bathroom, the second door, had only been partially repainted. Pink spots covered an old apple green. I sat on the seat stained with small dark yellow circles. The handle of the toilet flush was broken and patched up with duct tape. So much dirt had accumulated on the bathtub's enamel that the crud distorted its sides.

It was becoming urgent to show her where to start to lead a better life.

I washed my face and hands as best I could, without soap, without a hand towel. My features would have been better if I had used one of the makeup items that were spilling out of the pink and blue bags. My cheeks were pale, my eyelids swollen, my eyes wrinkled, my lips dry. Eleonore, of course, would one day see me in this state. But it was joy, calm, goodness, generosity that should emanate from my face today.

I opened the last door in the corridor. A corner floor lamp dimly lit the room. The dark blue curtains let a few rays of sunlight filter through. A double bed was in the middle of the room. Small tremors were shaking it.

One foot moved under the sheets and disappeared. Then three. One hand, then five, rounded shapes rising and falling. A deep groan, soft sighs, high-pitched sighs. A man's head came up from the chaotic and moving mass. A head with a wide smile on its face. Simon. Big sweaty Simon. At his side, two women.

I closed the door before they saw me. I went to sit in front of the TV.

I felt dizzy with fatigue.

Eleonore could not be responsible for this episode. There was no doubt about it. They had drawn her into it, and exhausted, she had gone along with it, finding it easier than to resist.

I pulled myself together.

I cleaned the apartment from top to bottom. I scrubbed the kitchen and bathroom. I transformed the living room into a pleasant, respectable place. I aired and perfumed the space with fresh air.

Eleonore was bound to thank me.

I waited until she came out of the room to make breakfast. Some canned fruit, sliced bread, blueberry jelly and yellow and white cheese.

They appeared as I was making coffee. Eleonore first. With her eyes distracted, she ducked off to the toilet without noticing me. Simon saw me. He was bare-chested. His belly stuck out. Black hair circled his nipples. A day-old beard covered his face.

– Well, well, well, he said, whistling between his lips. Behind him was one of the two redheads. She headed for the kitchen sink. She washed her hands and face for a long time, then sponged them with her t-shirt. Her actions were clumsy and fast. She put on her faded cotton jacket and left without even saying goodbye.

Eleonore came out of the bathroom and took a quick look at me.

– I don't recognize anything here anymore! It smells like household cleaning products.

She sat beside Simon, with her back to me, breathing a sigh of comfort. They exchanged a look. They looked at the full table and laughed. Simon leaned to her ear and started whispering something to her. Then he looked at me. He let out a few hums. She answered: "Yuck"!

She started cuddling his chest, whispering words in his ear, stuffing pieces of toast in his mouth, toast that she ordered me to prepare. I stayed near her for a while. She didn't seem to know how to spread the blueberry jelly on the bread or cut the cheese.

Then I opened all the windows and turned on the radio. They didn't notice when I started singing an old rock classic. I tried to forget about them. Be patient. He would leave and I would stay. I tried to immerse myself in a copy of *People Magazine* left out on the coffee table.

– There's still a room you haven't cleaned up!

I jumped up.

– Think carefully, she added.

She was right. She hadn't forgotten me. She needed me. She needed me. I had to take care of the backroom.

The sheets, duvet, pillows had been thrown to the ground. The mattress was uncovered and shifted from the box spring. A pungent, heavy, sharp smell lingered in the air. I cleaned everything up.

I took a rattan chair and put it in front of the wide-open closet. I sat there, closing my eyes, breathing in for a long time the fragrances that emanated from it. I went to lie down on the bed. I stayed there for a few minutes, enough time to imagine Eleonore and me together. Both of us in the country, laughing. Both of us in the dining room, confiding in each other. In the living room, holding hands, seized with fear as we watched an Alfred Hitchcock film.

I wanted Eleonore to remember my presence, that I was here, within these four walls. She needed to feel it when she came home to relax, to make herself beautiful or to meditate. Thoroughly cleaning everything up didn't seem to me to be enough. It was too neutral. Too far from life.

I scattered a few hairs ripped from my head under the pillow, on the floor, on the bedside table, between the sheets. I took off the shirt I was wearing under my sweater. I buried it in one of the drawers of her dresser. I took an old grocery bill out of my pocket and a pen from the bedside table.

My dear, you allowed me to enter your home. This is an important step in our relationship. I want you to know that I am fully aware of it. I will forever respect the pact that this permission establishes between us. Your friend who wants to be your best friend, Marianne N.

I put the piece of paper on the pillow, in plain sight. I checked one last time that everything was in order and then I exited the room with a perfect heart.

They had already left the apartment. I was alone in her place.

I noticed right away, on the kitchen table, a piece of paper under a ring with two keys. Two keys. At their rounded ends, an adhesive tape of a different colour, one pink, the other yellow. I felt them for a long time, between my index finger and my middle finger, between my thumb and my mouth afterwards. On the piece of paper were scribbled the words: "If you want."

Excited, I ate up everything left on the table. Bits of bread, cheese, a cup of apple sauce. I cleaned up, did the dishes. Eleonore had probably never had such a clean apartment before. I left locking the apartment door and then the building door with my two keys.

CHAPTER ELEVEN

I RETURNED THE next day and every day in the following weeks until mid-fall. I would come back to her place after work, and on the weekends in the early morning. Most of the time the apartment was empty. I would wait in the living room, watching TV. Or I would start to clean the house. I'd prepare meals with the groceries I had picked up along the way. I'd freeze them in small portions so that Eleonore would never find herself wanting.

Most of the time I was asleep when she came home. Since I woke up early to go to work, we only met on weekends. On Saturday morning, she left her room around one o'clock, with crazy hair, dull eyes or surprised to find me still there. She was always with someone. Never more than two people came out of the bedroom after her, but all the combinations were possible. A man or a woman, a man and a woman, two men or two women.

I made no comments about their hygiene or the way they talked. Instead, I hurried to prepare something for them to eat and told them about the day's news.

Eleonore remained silent. She used to spend a long time in the bathroom. When she came back to the dining room, she would eat a few crumbs. Then she would sit on the couch in the living room and start to smoke cigarette after cigarette, with or without her friends, always without me.

I used to write a few words on a piece of paper before I left. It was always more or less the same: "We'll see each other soon. Don't worry. I'll come back as quickly as I can, in the next few days. Your friend, Marianne."

I would leave her again my phone number and address, in case she had lost them. But she never needed to call me. I planned everything. I was reliable—reliable and loyal.

CHAPTER TWELVE

I HAD BEEN ABSENT from work several times since the end of the summer. I'd call in early in the morning and report a bad cold, indigestion or diarrhoea. The lies worked at first, but my colleagues' reactions to them gradually changed. I felt mistrust, odd and reproving looks.

Once stuck in the aquarium, I also understood that a connection had been broken with the patients. My usual caring for them had vanished. They had become vexatious obstacles who deliberately kept me from Eleonore. Work had become difficult.

In some cases, similarities between Eleonore and my patients would jump out. The same flat nose, hoarse voice, her way of giving evasive answers ...

There was a young woman, for example, who looked like Eleonore. She was a little older than her, but less damaged and more joyful despite the worries her broken arm caused her. I asked her the usual questions, according to the protocol I had always followed. But all my attention was focused on the fine folds that came from the corners of her eyes and ran deep into her hairline. She suspected something. I stared at her so hard. She lowered her head. She asked me in a trembling voice if she would be all right.

– It's just a broken arm! Nothing dangerous? You'll have to wait a while. Your case is not urgent, far from it!

With a scared look in her eyes, she shut up and left.

My impatience was worse with the next patient.

Something strong was emerging from him, something undeniable. But what? Irritation and hostility invaded me. I started shouting questions, pacing around the room, fiddling with his shin wound—a bloody wound. He muttered that he would wait in the waiting room, that I didn't have to worry about him. But I held him back with a firm arm and voice.

– Wait a minute! I'm going to disinfect this wound.

I took the opportunity to examine it in more detail.

– Tell me a little bit about yourself while I take care of all this. Are you a student?

He was a welder. He was older than students by a good ten years. I was confused.

He told me that he owned a welding shop with his brothers and that he had been injured while repairing a machine. For some reason, he laughed idiotically. And that's when I understood.

– Do you know a man named Simon? Fat, ugly, who laughs very loudly and sweats a lot?

He stopped laughing right away and stared at me.

– No. Are you almost done?

I pressed my thumb very hard on his wound.

41

He held back a cry of pain.

Distracted, I botched the rest and let him leave without adding anything. He looked worriedly at the loose bandage I left hanging around his calf.

With the last three patients, I completed the examination by saying to them: "You should have stayed home. You clutter up the emergency room by coming here with something so trivial!"

CHAPTER THIRTEEN

ONE LATE AFTERNOON, I met the receptionist. She was carrying a big cardboard box.

– You're re-decorating?

She had a wide and bright smile, which I had never seen before.

– Ah no! I'm leaving. I've had enough. I'm tired of their little boo-boos. They've been ruining my life! And I've been ruining the lives of all those around me. God! I've never felt better!

– But who will replace you?

She burst out laughing.

– I don't know and I don't care!

– You don't know who's going to replace you? You have no idea? Really?

She had no idea at all.

I thought of Eleonore's lost hours, so many, spent doing nothing. I thought about the state of her apartment, her fridge never full and her nights of excess and meaninglessness.

I took the elevator to the administration offices. After pressuring his secretary, I was able to enter the vast office of the Director of Human Resources. He was putting papers in a cheap leather case. I could sweeten him up for Eleonore.

— Good morning, sir. You probably don't recognize me, but I've been working in the emergency room for seven years. I apologize for coming without an appointment, just as your weekend is about to begin, but I have to talk to you.

He asked me to have a seat. He was young. He wanted to be liked by the staff.

— I just ran into the receptionist … the ex-receptionist, rather.

His face remained frozen in the same expression of exaggerated kindness.

— I suppose you're looking for someone to replace her as soon as possible?

— Do you have a recommendation?

— Yes! The ideal candidate. She's available right now.

He crossed his hands and legs, affected a calm look.

— It's very good to want to participate in the proper functioning of the hospital … yet you know that there is a rigorous process for hiring … that it's not as simple as you seem to think … of course, this is an exceptional situation … we don't have time to follow the usual procedure … yes, well, tell your contact to call me no later than Monday, 10 a.m.

I hurried to find Eleonore.

I found her sitting alone in her living room, watching a movie on TV. *Fatal Weapon 2*, I think it was.

A bowl of ramen noodles on her lap. A bottle of beer in her right hand.

She didn't react at all to my arrival.

– I have some great news!

I knelt in front of her. I took her plate and put it on the table behind me while leaving her the beer bottle.

– Listen to me. It's worth your while.

She took several sips, put her pillow on the floor and looked me right in the eye. Her eyes had fewer bags than usual.

I smiled with kindness.

– We're going to work in the same place, you and I. At the hospital!

I told her about the receptionist's departure, my conversation with the Director of Human Resources. I explained to her about the reception work—hospital reception, the schedule, pay, holidays …

– Can you imagine? We'll be able to go on holiday together, both of us for two weeks. You'll even have enough money to move … Come on! It doesn't cost you anything to try it out. If you don't like it, it's simple, you can quit.

She let out a hard laugh and got up to go to the bathroom.

– Aren't you going to answer me? Aren't you going to thank me? Are you going to call him?

I spent the evening waiting for a reaction from her. Nothing. She left the apartment shortly before midnight.

She wore a wig and perfume, high heels and thick layers of make-up. I went home.

CHAPTER FOURTEEN

I CALLED HER at home several times on Saturday and Sunday, but couldn't reach her.

Sunday evening, the day before the interview, I couldn't sleep. I had to swallow half of a sleeping pill at eleven, and the other half at one-thirty. I woke up the next day soaked in sweat. In the aquarium that Monday, I had trouble focusing on the descriptions patients gave me of their symptoms. The patients annoyed me. I quickly examined them and sent them back to the waiting room. I then went out to interrogate the nurses at the reception desk.

– Do you know if they've chosen a new receptionist?

They didn't know what I was talking about.

– Ah! Didn't you see the candidates go upstairs? One of them is remarkable: a little taller than me, about this high, with a pretty but tired face, a generous and adventurous look, and a lot more …

They were in a hurry. They didn't pay attention to my words. I headed back to my aquarium to receive the next patient.

At lunchtime, I went up to the administration offices. Everything was locked.

It occurred to me that Eleonore hadn't shown up. She would have greeted me otherwise. She betrayed me. She had not kept her word: to do everything to be hired as a receptionist at the hospital where I worked. How could she have refused such an opportunity? To get rich, to lead a stable, tidy life. To be at my side, almost every day. What kind of money was she living on?

At the end of the day, the manager entered the aquarium wearing a pink shirt and patent leather moccasins.

– I wanted to thank you. Eleonore is the perfect candidate! She will do very well. Thank you again. Your recommendation really helped us out.

I called her. The line was busy. The second, third, tenth time too. I gave up trying to reach her on the phone. I took a lot of money out of the ATM, a lot more than I usually carry with me. It was to celebrate Eleonore's new job, to invite her to a restaurant, the cinema, the theatre, anything she wanted to do.

I bought wine on the way, fine cheeses, a pack of Spanish deli meats, a baguette, a chocolate and raspberry cake. Over seventy-five dollars. Another twenty-five dollars for the taxi fare. I was proud: no one could pamper her so much.

I opened the door.

– Hey, Champ!

She was lying on the couch. Two empty beer bottles on the coffee table in front of her, a third half-drunk in her hand. The TV was turned down. Eleonore was staring at the ceiling. She stretched her neck to take a quick look at me.

I garnished a large plate with all my purchases. I cleaned up the living room table, where there were several days of garbage. I laid a navy blue cotton table-cloth and put on it two wine glasses and the bottle of sparkling wine in a Tupperware container filled with ice cubes and cold water.

– Come on! Let's celebrate! But not too much. Tomorrow's your first day!

I filled her glass to the brim. She got up and started drinking.

– Wait! We have to drink to something. Come on, you say it!

She began to blush terribly, as if something serious, forbidden, taboo was going to be revealed.

She whispered:

– I don't know about that … Cheers!

– Cheers! Dear friend …

We drank for several minutes without talking and looked around uncomfortably.

Then the phone rang. Eleonore jumped, rubbed her eyes and looked at me for a few seconds before answering it and returning to her usual attitude.

– Yes, right, I'm eating, drinking … I took your advice, showed up for the interview and got the job.

Laughter.

– Yes, it'll be a bit of money …

Laughter.

– No, I'm not alone, well, almost.

Laughter.

– Yes, come over right now. We'll have a little party. I'll wait, ciao!

She got up without looking at me, went to the bathroom, came back, put aside her glass of wine, opened a bottle of beer and guzzled down a third of it. Without saying a word, she left. Ten minutes later, she returned with a dozen cans of beer under her arm. I was still sitting in front of the living room table, which was covered with unopened packages of cheese.

She approached, opened a can and handed it to me.

– Come on, drink! Drink up!

Simon arrived a few minutes later, followed by a dozen people. They were noisy and already drunk. I was stunned by so much friendly indifference on their part. I started drinking.

Eleonore became playful and noisy. Nothing like she was earlier. She laughed loudly, was effusive, warm, touching everyone. I approached her, attempting to join the circle that had formed around her and that she animated with such talent. Everyone laughed at her jokes. Everyone looked at her with sparkling eyes. My friendship seemed ridiculous. Somebody suggested going downtown to continue the party. We all left together.

First, a billiards bar where I played and lost several games. There, we drank big pitchers of warm, bland beer. Simon and two of his sidekicks danced bare-chested on plastic stools. My eyes and legs started to wobble.

Then we took a long taxi ride to a nightclub in the east end. On the dance floor, Eleonore let herself go, dancing wildly in the middle of it. Men and women surrounded her, touched her, cutting her off from me. I don't know who filled my glass continuously, always to the brim with tonic and a lot of gin. I saw Eleonore's fury from afar. I tried to push through the dancers in front of me to join her. Dizziness, nausea, frustration overcame me. I threw up on their ankles and fell down.

I woke up alone the next day in my bed, still in my clothes.

I was very late for work. There were awful messages from my coordinator on my answering machine. I had to do everything to be excused, asking for a day off work, putting my colleagues in a difficult situation …

Had Eleonore reported for work? And in what condition?

CHAPTER FIFTEEN

WHEN I TOOK my place in the aquarium on Wednesday morning, Eleonore wasn't yet at her post. I went by the reception desk to ask the young man who was working there what time he would be replaced.

– In an hour. A new employee is taking over from me. She's just been hired and already she's getting the daytime shifts! I really don't understand their logic up there!

Eleonore was already disturbing the established order.

But I managed to concentrate on listening to my patients. The cases were always numerous and serious at the beginning of the week. I pushed away my thoughts of Eleonore who was a few steps away from me.

It was only in the middle of the morning that I was reminded of her presence. A colleague came to greet me and said, raising her eyebrows in a sideways glance.

– Did you see the new one they hired for the reception desk? Very tacky!

Other comments circulated in the afternoon:

– Did you see her clothes? What gall!

– She has a strange way of behaving and speaking for a person in charge of the reception!

– Where did they find this one?

No one was aware of the connection between Eleonore and me. No one knew that I was responsible for her hiring. I could not hold back a certain happiness: I liked it that Eleonore was not unanimously accepted. It would remind her how much she needed me.

She didn't come to see me in the aquarium. She probably didn't know where I worked. For my part, I was overwhelmed—I couldn't afford to take a detour to the reception desk. I wanted to meet her again when I had plenty of time to discuss and to help her. I left work without seeing her.

When I arrived home, after a shower and cup of tea, I sensed she wanted me to call her. I especially wanted to leave a message she would listen to and be comforted when she came home from work.

"Sometimes we get overwhelmed by the work, that's what happened to me today. That's why I couldn't come to see you. You understand, I said quietly, this work environment is not always easy. You don't have to worry about what your colleagues say. They are always like that when a new person tries to fit in. Don't worry. I'll always be by your side. I'll support you. You can count on me. I look forward to seeing you tomorrow. Good night!"

CHAPTER SIXTEEN

ELEONORE DIDN'T RETURN my call. I was happy and satisfied with the message I had recorded on her voice-mail. She'd appreciate it. This idea filled me with confidence.

– I can't believe the new one at the reception desk, a colleague told me at the ten o'clock break on Thursday morning. I felt a little pinch of pleasure in the middle of my chest.

The others would continue bad-mouthing her. It was my responsibility to protect her. My plan was to gradually inoculate them with the idea that Eleonore was a woman of value, of great quality. I would start at lunch-time, the time of day when gossiping is at its peak.

Just before noon, I took a look in the direction of the reception desk. I expected to see Eleonore overworked, a little panicky about the magnitude of the task, clumsily responding to several patients at once, making mistakes … I expected to see her in need. Instead, several colleagues were gathered around her and all were listening to her with wide smiles on their faces.

I arrived late in the dining room.

I took my lunch box out of the fridge. The usual complaints about working conditions, holidays, expensive restaurants were making the rounds. The litany went on for fifteen minutes before someone from the right corner of the table commented:

– Still, who would have thought they would hire such a person! Our bosses will always amaze me, really!

That was it. I had to fight to defend Eleonore's honour.

– Don't you like the new girl? But I saw you this morning, all gathered around her when the waiting room was spilling over with patients!

Under a leaden silence, all eyes turned to me. I had dared to criticize how they spent time at work. A colleague tried to calm things down.

– No, that's not what he meant. It's not like you dislike the new one, is it?

She managed to lighten the atmosphere undermined by my remark. Then to my great surprise, almost everyone began to praise Eleonore.

– Yes, I like her. She's, how I should say it, original? Special? And I'm surprised that the bosses hired her. That's all I meant!

In a chorus, the others said:

– Yes, yes, she's special!

Bursting out, they added:

– She makes us laugh!

– She's gutsy!

– She takes away the boredom!

– She puts rude patients in their place!

I retaliated:

– You're exaggerating a little! It's good if you see her positively, but you barely know her and you're already on your knees in front of her!

I didn't know what pushed me to make such a big thing of it.

– Like you know her more than we do! Relax!

The others, shaken by nervous laughter, looked into their plates.

– Well, yes, that's just it! I know her better than you do. I'm the reason she is working here. Eleonore and I are very good friends, I would even say that we are each other's best friend.

No one came to my rescue. I left, without saying goodbye. I spent the rest of the afternoon in a strange state as if I was at war.

At four o'clock, before leaving my post, I went to the reception desk. Eleonore heard my steps. She looked up. A strand of hair had come loose and fallen in front of her eyes. Some colleagues were having coffee a few steps away. They were watching us.

– Hello, Eleonore! See you later!

She squinted her eyes. She noticed the presence of the colleagues behind her and answered me:

– Hello … What department do you work in? Nice to meet you!

Our colleagues tried to hold back their laughs.

CHAPTER SEVENTEEN

IT CONTINUED LIKE THIS: Eleonore was a star, and I wasn't. I was mocked and then it seemed like we forgot about the episode. I returned to my previous status: an ordinary colleague, who is allowed to speak from time to time, to comment on the weather, the boss or fatigue. Only one or two colleagues continued to pass by to greet me, say a few words, ask me a question or two.

Eleonore never approached the aquarium. I stopped calling her. I didn't visit her anymore. I was waiting for her to calm down, to let her acknowledge her mistakes, to let her come back to me.

Then Eleonore disappeared. She disappeared in the late fall. Just after having revealed and confirmed our friendship once and for all during a meal with several other people present.

I knew she didn't eat often in the hospital. She preferred to go to one of the nearby cafés. But when she was at the table in the dining room, it was the event of the day! From the aquarium, I would see them leaving the dining room, all laughing and in a crazy good mood.

This time, there were several of us and, exceptionally, Eleonore was present. For reasons I don't know, she had started earlier that day, with the seven o'clock group of workers.

The retirement of a nurse was the topic of the meal.

— She's truly earned her retirement, after so many years in the operating room!

— To think that she had to put up with Dr. Vézina and his horrible breath day after day!

— She's lucky, retiring after only twenty years of service. That's not likely to happen for us!

Eleonore whispered something to her neighbours on the left. One of them burst out laughing, loud enough to interrupt the main conversation and attract everyone's attention.

— We want to know, we want to laugh too! Come on, tell us!

Eleonore repeated the joke. The people around her added a few details. I didn't pay attention. I wasn't listening. I was very far away, withdrawn. I despised others for being so attached to her. Then Eleonore said:

— Marianne and I have been there together before. Haven't we, Marianne?

She asked this in front of everyone. She spoke to me directly in the presence of those who had laughed at me. She brought up a common past between the two of us, and in front of everyone.

The faces turned to me, surprised at my sudden importance.

Without waiting for me to answer, someone asked:

– So, you two know each other? For how long?

Hypocrite! As if I hadn't already told him.

Eleonore smiled.

– Yes, of course, we know each other. Didn't you know that?

She turned to me:

– Isn't that right, Marianne? And we have known each other for quite a while! One of these days, we will tell you our story and how we met. There are a lot of amusing things to say about it.

My ears were ringing. Faces and eyes were turned towards me. Then the conversation started up again with another subject.

CHAPTER EIGHTEEN

I HAVEN'T SEEN her since that meal. Neither have our other colleagues.

When she didn't come back to work the next day, we first thought it was amusing. We blamed this absence on her audacity, her freedom. In the following days, the indulgence decreased. Practical problems began to emerge. Who would replace her? We were so close to the Christmas holidays.

– I'm not going to do any overtime this time. They just have to manage up there to find reliable people!

– Yes! People who don't leave right after making a little money!

Some colleagues asked me if I knew anything about it. Where was Eleonore hiding? Why didn't she answer the phone and return the calls?

The weeks passed, we found a replacement and the memories became confused. When it came to Eleonore, in my presence, people laughed at the "old newbie," who dressed grotesquely, made lame jokes, which often cross the line, and even went as far as frightening patients and disturbing the peace they needed for their recovery.

CHAPTER NINETEEN

JUST AFTER CHRISTMAS about two weeks following her disappearance from work and after calling her home every day several times and knocking on her door also several times, I began to look for her in earnest. Her friends, the ones I had met at the apartment and others I approached in the bars I knew Eleonore frequented, all said that they had seen her increasingly less in recent weeks.

– She's been "intense" lately!

I was told that she spent a lot of money in bars, that she often paid for everyone, that she got drunk every night and brought several guests home to spend the night. I was terribly sorry I hadn't tried to reach out to her sooner.

I explored and searched the streets she frequented. I asked everyone about her. One tried to reassure me:

– She always comes back. It's not the first time she's vanished like this. There's no point in notifying the police.

All I could do was wait and be patient. And that's what I did.

CHAPTER TWENTY

I MOVED INTO her apartment. I sublet mine to one of my colleagues' brothers. It would be easier that way when Eleonore returned.

Her landlord came by one day. He was furious and threatened to empty the apartment, throw away Eleonore's belongings and rent it to someone else if she did not pay her rent in person. I argued that I had settled everything, that Eleonore was not in debt to him, but he wouldn't listen. He repeated that Eleonore was the one responsible for the apartment. She was the one who had signed the lease.

One March evening when I came home later than usual, I saw about fifteen enormous garbage bags lined up and stacked along the sidewalk. The rod and curtains of Eleonore's living room stuck out of one of them. I looked up and saw that her windows were bare. I climbed the stairs at full speed to the apartment. The owner was coming out of it with a smile on his face.

– I warned you about this! It's been over three months and it's my right to evict her.

I tried everything to convince him. He kept shaking his head, smiling.

– Goodbye, Madam! We do what we can in life. We have to survive in this difficult world. I don't have a choice …

He slammed the door behind him, passed in front of me and ran down the stairs. I waited a while in shock. I tried to open the door. He had changed the lock. I couldn't go in there anymore. Eleonore could never come back home.

I called a taxi and filled it with as many garbage bags as I could. I rented a hotel room for a week while my colleague's brother vacated my apartment.

CHAPTER TWENTY-ONE

BACK HOME, I redesigned everything so that Eleonore wouldn't feel out of place when she came back. The chair here, the TV there. I replaced the bedding. I repainted and found a coffee table that looked like hers. I changed the curtains.

I threw away my clothes and replaced them with Eleonore's clothes. Eleonore being much thinner than me, there were only a few that fit me, mostly sweatsuits. But they are now the ones that made up my wardrobe. That's what I wear now.

In the evening, I sometimes drink one of the beers from the case, which I regularly renew for the moment when Eleonore will knock on my door.

I've also been going to one of the bars she frequented and the last time I came home with a stranger who left in the early morning hours.

While I wait for her, while she searches for me.

AUTHOR

ANDRÉE A. GRATTON was born in Arvida, Quebec in 1980. After studying philosophy and classical studies in Montreal, Berlin and Strasbourg, she became a philosophy professor in Montreal. *Choisir Éléonore*, published by Editions de la Pleine Lune, is her first novel. It was a finalist for the Grand Prix Littéraire Archambault and the winner of the Découverte Prize of the Salon du livre du Saguenay-Lac-St-Jean. In 2019, she contributed a short story to the *Enfances Plurielles* anthology, published by Éditions de la Pleine Lune. Gratton is currently working on her second novel. She loves running, swimming in cold water and all the nuances of the colour green.

TRANSLATOR

IAN THOMAS SHAW is a novelist, translator and editor. Born in Vancouver, British Columbia in 1955, he has lived in Quebec and abroad since 1977. He has previously translated *The Unending Journey (El viajé interminable)* by Chilean-Canadian author José Del Pozo Artigas (Editorial Mapalé 2019) and published two novels: *Soldier, Lily, Peace and Pearls* (Deux Voiliers Publishing 2013) and *Quill of the Dove* (Guernica Editions 2019). Shaw is a former Canadian diplomat and for many years lived in Europe, Africa and the Middle East. He speaks English, French, German, Spanish and some Arabic.